American Pokeberry
(Phytolacca americana)

Interrupted Fern
(Osmunda claytoniana)

Pumpkin, Squash
(Cucurbita genus)

Bronze frog
(Rana clamitans)

Velvet Parachute Mushroom
(Marasmius elegans)

Garter snake
(Thamnophis genus)

Okra
(Abelmoschus esculentus)

Little Brown Bat
(Myotis lucifugus)

Trumpet Honeysuckle
(Lonicera sempervirens)

Sweet potato
(Ipomoea batatas)

Monarch chrysalis
(Danaus plexippus)

Ruby-throated Hummingbird
(Archilochus colubris)

Field mouse
(Family muridae)

Milkweed
(Asclepias syriaca)

Earthworm
(Lumbricus genus)

Rhododendron
(Rhododendron ponticum)

In the Garden with Dr. Carver

Susan Grigsby   illustrated by Nicole Tadgell

Albert Whitman & Company, Chicago, Illinois

To Perry, with love—SG

In memory of my grandfather, T. H. Boykin,
who stirred in his daughter and granddaughters
the love for making things grow—NT

CULTURAL WAGON

I'll never forget the Sunday that we stepped out of church and saw an old mule waiting beside a funny-looking wagon.

The man with the wagon was George Washington Carver, the famous plant scientist from the big school in Tuskegee.

Dr. Carver called the wagon his movable school, and it was piled high with plants, tools, and seeds.

The adults all gathered around, eager for advice. They had heard about the twenty-pound cabbages and the onions as big as a young child's head that Dr. Carver had grown on land just like ours. He said that plants get from the soil the foods that they need to make them grow. But cotton, like a hungry monster, had gobbled up the good foods in Alabama's soil. Dr. Carver was showing folks how to make our poor soil healthy again.

He was even teaching people how to turn
simple foods like peanuts and sweet potatoes into
luxuries like coffee, butter, and sugar. Hundreds of
new products poured out of his laboratory, all made
from plants that we could grow.

But for me, the best part of Dr. Carver's visit was that he agreed to stay through Monday to help us with the garden at our school.

"Who here would like to learn to be a plant doctor?" Dr. Carver asked.

I waved my hand the hardest, so he asked me to observe the first case.

"So, Dr. Sally," he said, "why do you think that this rosebush is looking so weak, when her cousins by the fence are covered in beautiful red roses?"

"I don't know," I admitted. "What should I do first?"

"Listen to the plants, and they'll tell you what they need. Go on."

I thought about what Dr. Carver meant. Maybe it was like listening to the wind and watching the sky to tell the weather.

I looked over at the healthy roses, basking in the bright sunshine. Then I examined my patient. Just one single rose grew on her entire bush, as she sat all alone in the shade beside the shed.

"I've got it!" I cried out. "My patient needs to be moved to where she'll get more sunlight."

"That is an excellent job of observation, Dr. Sally," Dr. Carver said. "Now, let us begin the operation."

Dr. Carver showed us how to transplant the rosebush, very carefully, without damaging her roots or letting her scratch us.

Common whitetail
(Libellula lydia)

Oxeye daisy
(Leucanthemum vulgare Lam.)

Honey Bee
(Apis mellifera)

American tree sparrow
(Spizella arborea)

"When I was a boy," said Dr. Carver, "drawing and plants were my two passions. I mixed my own paints and covered stones and discarded boards with pictures of the flowers. And I was always asking questions. I wanted to know the names of every strange stone and flower, every insect, bird, and beast that visited the garden."

We wanted to know all about the garden, too. So we just sat there, quiet, watching, listening to Nature, and drawing the beetles and bees, flowers and fungi, worms and birds and pretty bits of stones. I never knew our garden was such a busy place!

And Dr. Carver knew the names of everything.

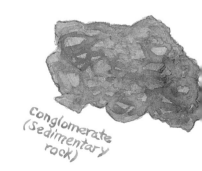
Quaking Aspen
(Populus tremuloides)

Red Maple
(Acer rubrum)

May Beetle
(Phyllophaga species)

American Painted Lady Butterfly
(Vanessa virginensis)

Field cricket
(Gryllus pennsylvanicus)

Conglomerate
(Sedimentary rock)

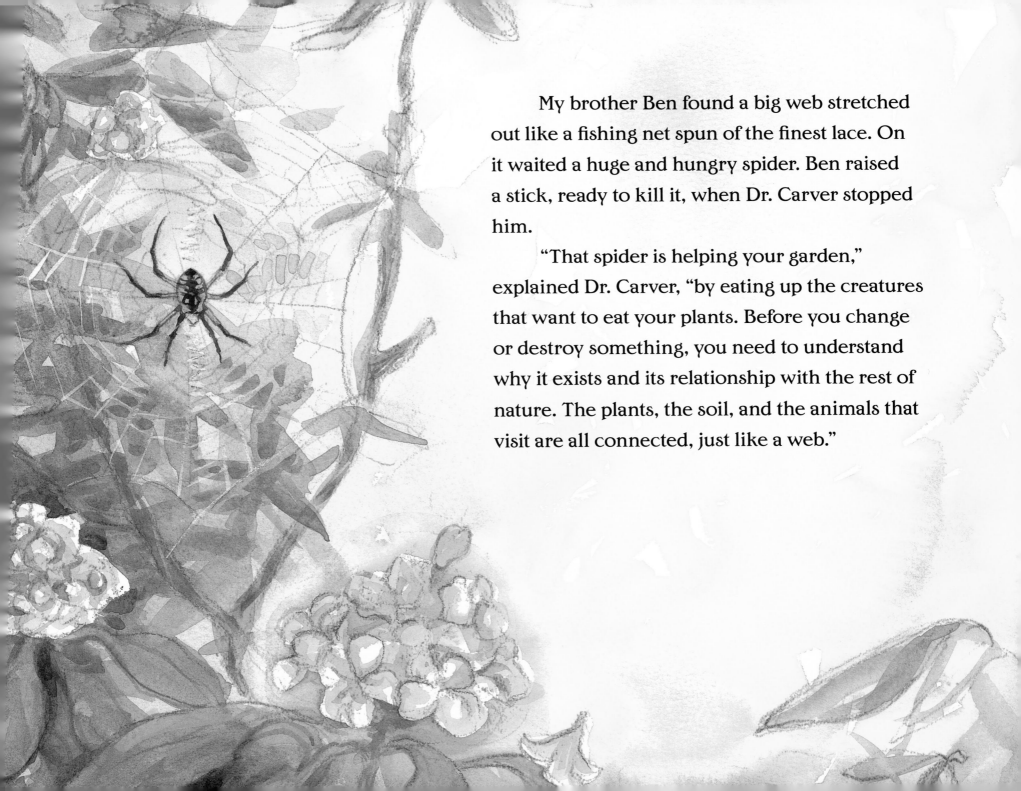

My brother Ben found a big web stretched out like a fishing net spun of the finest lace. On it waited a huge and hungry spider. Ben raised a stick, ready to kill it, when Dr. Carver stopped him.

"That spider is helping your garden," explained Dr. Carver, "by eating up the creatures that want to eat your plants. Before you change or destroy something, you need to understand why it exists and its relationship with the rest of nature. The plants, the soil, and the animals that visit are all connected, just like a web."

In every single flowerbed, dandelions held up their sunny yellow heads.

"Who planted all of these?" Lucy asked.

"That would be Old Man Wind," chuckled Dr. Carver. He showed us how the fluff of a dandelion puffball was really a family of hundreds of seeds. Carried by the wind, they could travel miles before landing and beginning to grow.

A plant is a weed if it's growing uninvited, we learned. Those greedy dandelions were taking food, light, and water from the flowers that our teacher, Miss Simpson, had planted. Dr. Carver showed us how to remove the dandelions, pulling them up by their long and hungry roots.

We saved their youngest leaves for our lunchtime salad. Dr. Carver said that we should eat all of the fruits and vegetables that we could.

By then, we were as hungry as a pack of wild dandelions! Miss Simpson and the older students had cooked a delicious spread of picnic food using recipes invented by Dr. Carver. After every bit was gobbled up, they told us what we'd eaten—sweet-potato-flour bread, "chicken" made from peanuts, and a salad of strange wild weeds. And for dessert—peanut ice cream and cake!

After our feast, Dr. Carver said that it was time to plant our own kitchen garden. We followed him to the lot behind our school.

"This spot is no good," Emmett said. "It's sunny, but the soil's rock-hard. See, it won't budge."

"He's right," I said. "Nothing ever grows out here, not even weeds."

"And nothing ever will, unless we improve this worn-out land," said Dr. Carver. "Plants, like people, need nutritious food to help them grow."

Dr. Carver took us to a patch of forest near our school. We scooped up buckets full of rich and leafy loam. While we worked, he explained how rotting plants were full of good things to feed healthy plants.

"Leaf mulch, swamp muck, and the decaying roots of peanuts, peas, and beans will all enrich the soil," he said. "You can make your own fertilizer, too. I'll leave Miss Simpson my recipe for compost. Paper shreds, vegetable scraps, anything that breaks down quickly will put nutrients back into the soil. So much of what people waste can be put to good use."

We cleared the plot of stones, spaded and hoed, chopped and raked, turning and mixing into the soil the forest humus we'd gathered. We worked that soil until we had a fine rich field. Then we divided it into plots. We planted sweet potato slips and peanuts, snap beans, lima beans, cowpeas, squash, okra, and melons.

Dr. Carver asked us to show him the nearest dump. We found wood scraps to use for our plant markers and a raggedy-headed mop to make a tall scarecrow. When Clarence grumbled about picking through the dump, Dr. Carver told us how he'd made test tubes, lamps, and all sorts of tools for his laboratory from the re-used treasures of just such a dump. The word "treasure" set Clarence's eyes on fire, and he kept picking until he found a fine costume for our shaggy-headed scarecrow.

Back at school, we used milk paint to label our garden signs so that we'd remember what we'd planted, where.

We were all sad to see Dr. Carver leave. But he made Miss Simpson promise to take us outdoors every day for nature study and gardening lessons, and he gave her papers he'd written, to use as our school guides.

And we promised Dr. Carver that we wouldn't eat wild weeds, as some can be very poisonous, until our teacher taught us which ones were safe.

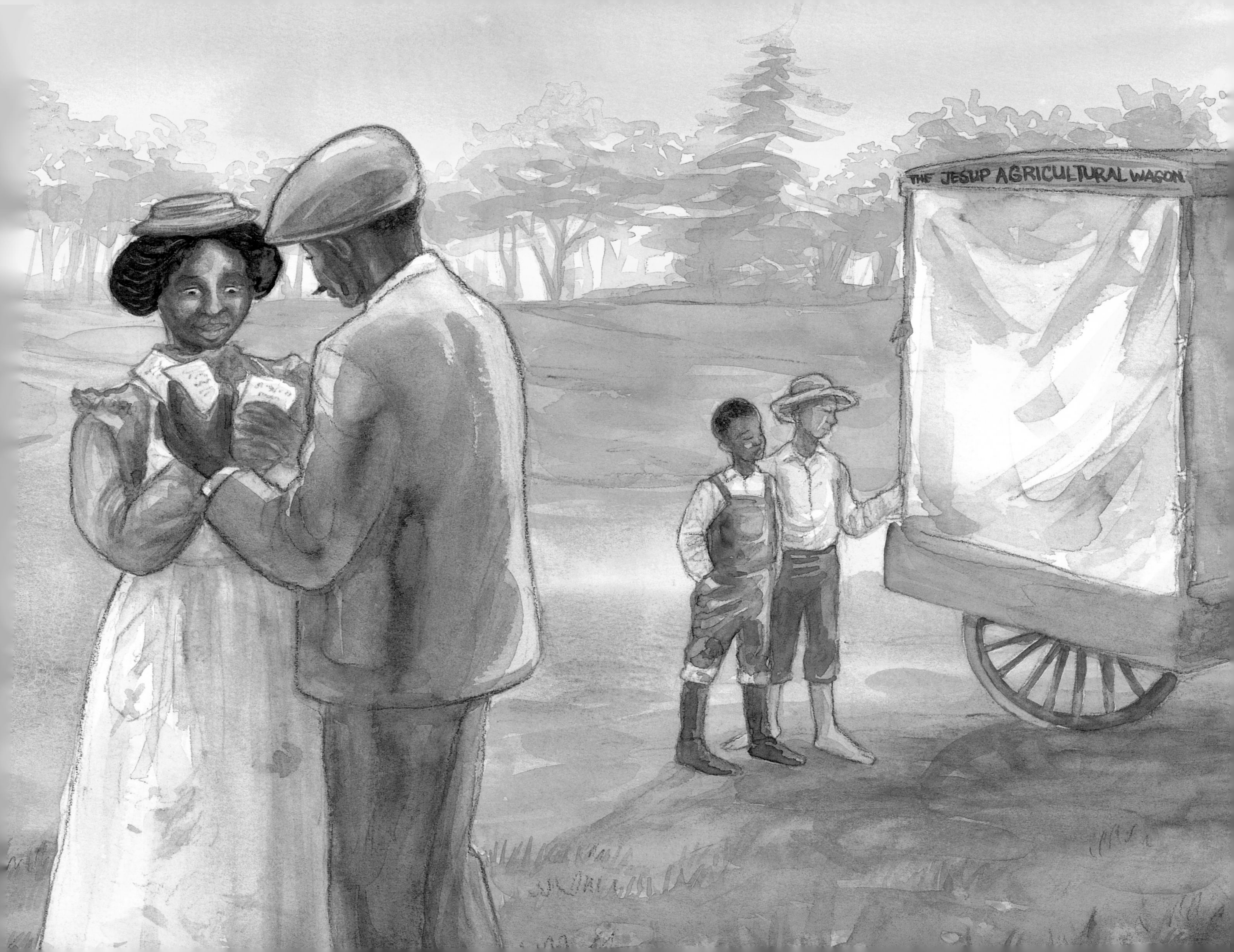
THE JESUP AGRICULTURAL WAGON

Some people come in and out of your life, as quick as a hummingbird darting at a trumpet vine. And some of them, when gone, leave something behind that sticks in your heart or mind. It sticks to you like a little burr on your sock. It wraps around you like the tendrils of a vine.

Since that day that we spent in the garden with Dr. Carver, whenever I step among flowers, trees, or vegetables, I remember his words.

Listen to the plants, and they'll tell you what they need.

And they do.

This story is historical fiction. It is based on the history of Dr. George Washington Carver and his writings.

Dr. Carver was born into slavery on a Missouri farm, about a year before slavery was abolished. He spent his early years seeking out schools and learning all they offered. He taught botany at Iowa State College while earning a master's degree in agricultural science. In 1896, Booker T. Washington asked Dr. Carver to be the head of the Department of Agriculture at the Tuskegee Institute in Alabama. Dr. Carver worked there until his death in 1943.

Dr. Carver dedicated his life to helping people improve their lives by working with what nature provided. In addition to teaching the students at Tuskegee, he wanted to help the farmers across the South. He wrote many bulletins to teach people how to take care of the earth, how to farm, and how to make the things they needed. He also wrote booklets for teachers, explaining ways to conduct nature studies in the schools.

But Dr. Carver realized that many people would learn best by being shown what to do. So on weekends, using an old wagon pulled by a mule, Dr. Carver took a movable school out into the Alabama countryside to teach. In 1906, he outfitted a better wagon and called it the Jesup Wagon after Mr. Morris K. Jesup who donated the money for it. By 1918, he was using a truck.

Dr. Carver's idea of movable schools was adapted in places as far away as China and India.

The research for this book was enriched by the resources and the staff assistance at the Missouri Botanical Garden, St. Louis, Missouri; the Graduate School of Education, Webster University, St. Louis, Missouri; and the Tuskegee Institute National Historic Site, Tuskegee, Alabama. Special acknowledgment is also due the Missouri History Museum, St. Louis, Missouri, and the Field Museum's George Washington Carver exhibition, Chicago, Illinois.

Library of Congress Cataloging-in-Publication Data

Grigsby, Susan.
In the garden with Doctor Carver / Susan Grigsby ; illustrated by Nicole Tadgell.
p. cm.
Summary: A fictionalized account of how plant scientist George Washington Carver came to an Alabama school and taught the children how to grow plants and reap the rewards of nature's bounty. Includes factual note about George Washington Carver.
1. Carver, George Washington, 1864?–1943—Juvenile fiction. [1. Carver, George Washington, 1864?–1943—Fiction. 2. Garden ecology—Fiction.
3. Gardening—Fiction. 4. Schools—Fiction. 5. African Americans—Fiction.] I. Tadgell, Nicole, ill. II. Title.
PZ7.G88418In 2010 [E]—dc22 2009048124

Peanut
(Arachis hypogaea)

Oxeye daisy
(Leucanthemum vulgare Lam.)

Honey Bee
(Apis mellifera)

American tree sparrow
(Spizella arborea)

Conglomerate
(Sedimentary
rock)

Quaking Aspen
(Populus tremuloides)

Monarch butterfly
caterpillar
(Danaus plexippus)

Common dandelion
(Taraxacum officinale)

Rose
(Rosa 'Gloire Des
Rosomanes')

Yellow garden spider
(Argiope aurantia)

Magnolia
(Magnolia grandiflora)

Red Maple
(Acer rubrum)

May Beetle

(Phyllophaga species)

American Painted Lady Butterfly
(Vanessa virginiensis)

Field cricket
(Gryllus pennsylvanicus)

Common whitetail

(Libellula

lydia)